DEDICATION

To the magic of every smile!

ACKNOWLEDGMENTS

I would like to send a giant smile of thanks to:

Gary Peattie for all his belief in spreading this message around the world . . .

To Jana Christy for the smile that shines in her beautiful illustrations . . .

To my son Elijah for everything that he is and a love that cannot

be explained with words . . .

To Coco and Jojo who have the greatest doggie smiles in the whole world . . .

To my friends far and wide and their smiles that will always live inside of me . . .

To the Divine Spirit of the Universe--The great Smile that is felt by all . . .

And mostly . . .

To you, the children of the world. Never forget the magic of your smile!

PUBLISHER'S DEDICATION

To Marianne, the smile that went to heaven.

The Smile that went Around the World

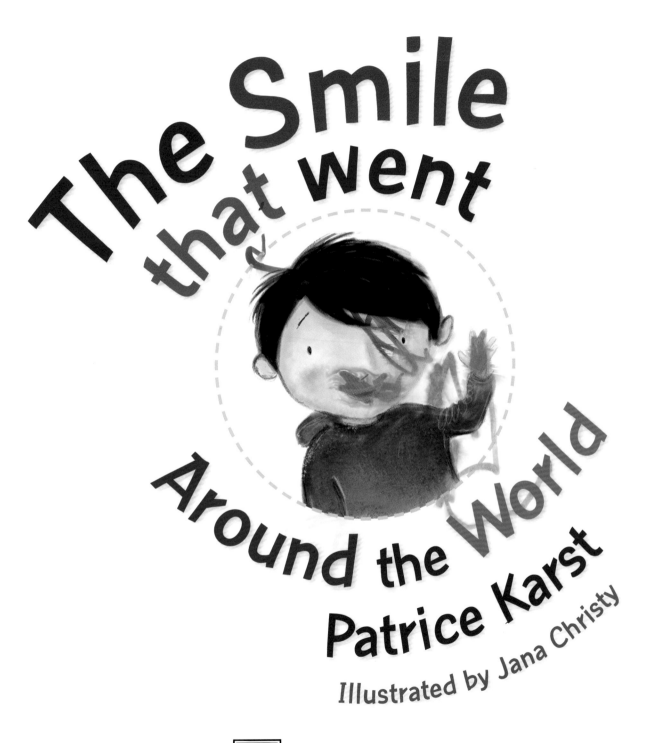

Patrice Karst

Illustrated by Jana Christy

DeVorss Publications

www.devorss.com

The Smile That Went Around the World

Text Copyright © 2009 by Patrice Karst

Illustrations Copyright © 2009 by Jana Christy

ISBN: 978-087516-875-3

Library of Congress Catalog Card Number: 2007920404

First Edition, 2009
Second Edition, 2014

Printed in Canada

Cover and Book Design by Michelle Farinella Design
Author Photo by Angela Paul

DeVorss & Company, Publishers
PO Box 1389
Camarillo CA 93011-1389
www.devorss.com

This is a story about a smile . . .

. . . that went around the world.

🌼 1

Justin and his mother were on their way to a party.
In the backseat, Justin carefully held a big plate of
cookies as they passed the bike store and some
people waiting for a bus.

4

At the very next corner, Justin saw some people standing in a doorway who looked cold and sad. One of them held a sign that said PLEASE HELP, WE ARE HUNGRY.

"Mommy, I wish we could give the cookies to those people, they are very hungry." His mother thought for a minute then said, "I think there will be enough food at the party. Yes, let's share the cookies."

So she parked the car, walked over and handed them the whole plate of cookies. That's when Justin rolled down his window and yelled, "You're going to LOVE our cookies. They're rainbow sprinkled, my favorite kind!"

This made Justin smile and feel good inside.

7

As Justin and his mom drove to the party
he felt so good that he waved and smiled
to all the other people along the road.

They all smiled and waved back . . . except
for Rupert Price in his blue car.

9

When he got closer, Rupert Price saw Justin smiling and waving.

That made him smile as he drove to the airport to catch his plane to Hong Kong.

When Rupert Price got on the plane
he saw a lady having trouble with her bag.

He smiled, jumped out of his seat and said,
"I'll help you with that."

"Well, thank you ever so much!" said Mrs. Green
as they smiled at each other.

It didn't take long for Justin's smile to spread faster and faster.

After it went from Rupert Price to Mrs. Green, it went to all the people they met after that. From young people to old people. From happy people to lonely people. From rich people to poor people. From farmers market people to little baby stroller people. From tall people to short people . . . and even in-between people.

✿ 15

Then something very interesting happened.

One day, Justin was at soccer practice and not playing very well.

Coach Martinez could see that Justin was unhappy so he smiled and asked him if he'd like to work on his kicking after practice.

"Sure," said Justin, and in only a few minutes he was kicking the ball better and feeling excited about the next game.

18 ❀

Afterwards, Coach Martinez walked Justin home and asked him what he liked to do for fun besides soccer.

"I like to ride bikes with my dad and shoot hoops with mom. What do you like to do Coach?"

"I like to run, go to the beach with my family, and fly airplanes." Coach then said, "Did you know that I'm an airline pilot?"

"That sounds really fun!" said Justin.

"It is. I meet people from all over the world. Last week I flew to Hong Kong and a very nice lady with a beautiful smile told me it was a great flight. That made me smile and feel good inside."

At that moment, Justin had received a very special gift . . .
    . . . but he didn't even know it.

Remember the smile that Justin felt in his heart when he shared the cookies? Well here's what happened to that smile.

Justin gave it to . . .

Rupert Price, who gave it to . . .

Mrs. Green,
who took it all the way
to Hong Kong and gave it to . . .

Coach Martinez, who flew it back home and gave it to . . .

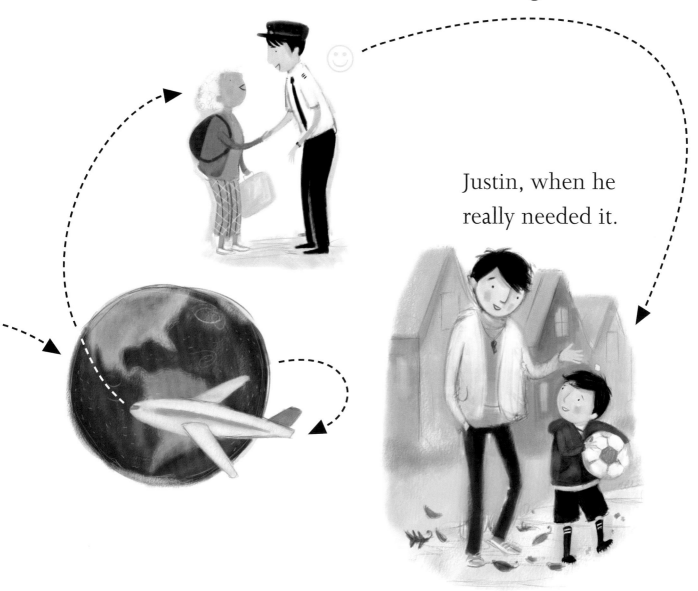

Justin, when he really needed it.

You see, the smile that went around the world started in Justin's very own heart!

You never really know how far a smile can go.
When one comes your way, it may have traveled
thousands of miles and cheered millions of people
before it ever reached you.

But even more amazing than that, just think about
how far your next smile might go!